THE KATIE LYNN COOKIE COMPANY

PRESIDENT: KATIE LYNN
VICE PRESIDENT: TINA
HEAD BAKER: GRANDMA

AGENDA:

1. FIND OUT IF GRANDMA IS GIVING AWAY COMPANY SECRETS.

2. SHOW EVERYONE—ESPECIALLY JONATHAN WILBARGER—THAT WE'RE THE BEST BAKERS IN TOWN.

3. WIN THE SECRET GRAND PRIZE AT THE BATTLE OF THE BAKERS.
   (HA! TAKE THAT, JONATHAN!)

To Shana, for making everything work so well—
and to
Gwen, Charles, James, and Tambye,
with all my love!

Text copyright © 2000 by G. E. Stanley.
Illustrations copyright © 2000 by Linda Dockey Graves.
All rights reserved under International and Pan-American Copyright
Conventions. Published in the United States of America by Random House, Inc.,
New York, and simultaneously in Canada by Random House of Canada Limited,
Toronto.

www.randomhouse.com/kids

Library of Congress Cataloging-in-Publication Data
Stanley, George Edward.
Battle of the bakers / by George Edward Stanley ;
illustrated by Linda Dockey Graves.
p. cm. — (The Katie Lynn Cookie Company ; #3)
"A Stepping Stone Book."
Summary: Katie Lynn and Tina are sure they will win the town's bake-off, until
Jonathan Wilbarger enters the contest and the competition starts to heat up.
ISBN 0-679-89222-2 (trade). — ISBN 0-679-99222-7 (lib. bdg.)
[1. Baking—Fiction. 2. Competition (Psychology)—Fiction. 3. Grandmothers—
Fiction.] I. Graves, Linda, ill. II. Title.
PZ7.S78694Bat 2000 [Fic]—dc21 99-18952
Printed in the United States of America
November 2000   10 9 8 7 6 5 4 3 2 1

The Katie Lynn Cookie Company

#3

THE
Battle
of the Bakers

by **G. E. Stanley**

illustrated by Linda Dockey Graves

A STEPPING STONE BOOK™
Random House 🏠 New York

Contents

1. The Contest   1

2. Who's That Man?   9

3. Grandma Invites the Enemy Home 16

4. Disaster!   23

5. Ready for Battle   35

6. Bakers, Get Ready!   39

7. Mixing Bowl Mix-up   48

8. Chocolate-Buttermilk Bread   56

   Katie Lynn's Cookbook   69

Chapter 1

The Contest

Katie Lynn looked around the library to see if any of the other kids were watching her. They weren't.

She took the flyer out of her pocket and unfolded it. In big letters, it said:

BATTLE OF THE BAKERS
Sponsored by the Better Cooks Flour Company!

A baking contest for students in grades one through four!

Win a secret grand prize!

1

In smaller letters, it explained the rules.

Their teacher, Mrs. Nattison, had given a flyer to everyone in their class. Everyone thought that the secret grand prize was a million dollars. Some of the kids planned to enter the contest. But Katie Lynn and Tina were sure they could beat them.

After all, they had been baking cookies for the Katie Lynn Cookie Company for a long time. What would their customers think if they *didn't* win?

Katie Lynn pulled a cookbook off the shelf.

All of a sudden, Tina whispered, "Katie Lynn! There he is!"

Katie Lynn quickly turned. Tina had pulled several cookbooks off the shelf. Now she was looking through the empty space to the other side.

"Tina!" said Katie Lynn. "What are you doing?"

Tina giggled. "I'm spying on Jonathan Wilbarger!"

"Jonathan Wilbarger?" Katie Lynn gasped. "Why are you spying on him?"

"Because I think he's cute," replied Tina.

"Really?" said Katie Lynn. "You never told me that before. Let me look!"

Tina moved over.

Jonathan was sitting alone at a library table. He was reading a book.

Katie Lynn turned back to Tina. "I agree."

Tina frowned. "You do?"

Katie Lynn nodded. "I think he's the cutest boy in our class!"

She looked through the bookshelf

again. Now she saw Mrs. Nattison's face looking back.

"Katie Lynn Cooke!" said Mrs. Nattison. "What are you doing?" Mrs. Nattison came around the end of the bookshelf. "Haven't you girls picked out your books yet?" she asked.

"Yes, ma'am," said Tina. She held up her book.

Katie Lynn quickly grabbed a book off the shelf. "Yes, ma'am," she said.

"Then please start reading," said Mrs. Nattison. "Library time is almost over." She pointed to Jonathan's table. "Sit over there," she said.

Tina looked at Katie Lynn and grinned.

They walked over to Jonathan's table.

"We have to sit with you, Jonathan," Tina said. "Mrs. Nattison said so."

Jonathan shrugged. "Okay."

Katie Lynn and Tina pulled out their chairs and sat down.

"What book did you pick out to read?" asked Tina.

Jonathan held up the book for them to see. "It's about bread."

"Bread?" said Tina.

"Your family owns a bakery, Jonathan," said Katie Lynn. "Don't you already know about bread?"

"I want to look for new recipes," said Jonathan.

"Why?" asked Katie Lynn.

"I'm going to enter the Battle of the Bakers," Jonathan said. "I'm going to win the secret grand prize."

"No way!" Tina cried. "We are!"

"Boys don't even know how to cook," said Katie Lynn.

"Are you kidding? All the best chefs are guys," said Jonathan. "Some restaurants don't even hire girls."

"What about Mr. Chesterfield's restaurant?" said Katie Lynn. "We bake *his* cookies!"

"Yeah, Jonathan!" said Tina. "What have *you* ever baked?"

"Bread," Jonathan replied. He grinned. "Lots and lots of bread. I started helping Dad and Grandpa when I was a little kid."

Katie Lynn and Tina looked at each other.

"Grandma bought some bread at your bakery the other day," said Katie Lynn. "Did you help bake that?"

"Probably," Jonathan said. "Did you like it?"

Katie Lynn shrugged. "It was okay."

"What do you mean 'okay'?" Jonathan said. "It's the best bread in town."

"Time to go, class!" Mrs. Nattison announced.

Jonathan stood up. "My bread is going to beat your cookies," he said. He started toward the door.

"Our cookies are going to beat your bread!" Katie Lynn called after him.

"Boys!" said Tina. "Sometimes they really make me mad."

"I know," said Katie Lynn.

Then Tina sighed dreamily. "But I still think he's cute," she said.

"So do I," said Katie Lynn.

Chapter 2

Who's That Man?

Katie Lynn and Tina ran down the sidewalk toward Katie Lynn's house.

"I don't care how cute Jonathan is," said Katie Lynn. "We just can't let him win the Battle of the Bakers! We need to talk to Grandma right away!"

"Why?" asked Tina.

"She knows more cooking secrets than any book," said Katie Lynn. "She can help us choose just the right cookie recipe to beat Jonathan!"

"Won't that be cheating?" Tina asked.

"No. You can talk to a grownup *before* the battle," replied Katie Lynn. "But during the battle, the only thing they can do is turn on the oven and take out the cookies."

"Oh, then that's a great idea!" said Tina. "With your grandmother behind us, there's no way Jonathan will win!"

But when they reached the corner of their block, Katie Lynn suddenly stopped. "Tina! There's Grandma!" she said. "She's with a *man!*"

"Who is it?" Tina said.

"I can't see his face," said Katie Lynn.

They watched as Grandma and the man went inside Katie Lynn's house.

"Come on!" said Katie Lynn.

They hurried up the porch steps and through the front door. Inside, they could hear Grandma and the man laughing in the kitchen.

"Grandmas aren't supposed to act like that," said Tina.

"I know," said Katie Lynn. "But she's been acting strange for a while now."

"I wonder what they're laughing about," said Tina. They started toward the kitchen door. It was open slightly.

Grandma and the man were sitting at the kitchen table. They were drinking coffee. The man had his back to the door.

Katie Lynn opened the door the rest of the way. It made a loud squeaking noise.

Grandma jumped. "Katie Lynn! Tina! Goodness! You startled me!" she said.

The man turned around.

Katie Lynn and Tina gasped. It was Jonathan Wilbarger's grandfather!

"Hello, girls," Mr. Wilbarger said.

"Hello," Katie Lynn and Tina said.

Why is Grandma talking to Jonathan's grandfather? Katie Lynn wondered. *He's the enemy!*

"I've been hearing all about your company," said Mr. Wilbarger. "Your cookies are wonderful."

Uh-oh! Katie Lynn thought. She wondered exactly how much Mr. Wilbarger had heard. She hoped they had gotten there before Grandma could tell him anything important.

"Thank you," said Katie Lynn. "We like your bread."

Mr. Wilbarger smiled.

"I understand you girls are going to enter the Battle of the Bakers. Jonathan is, too," said Mr. Wilbarger. "He's really excited about it. He thinks his bread will win."

"We think our cookies will win," said Katie Lynn.

Grandma winked at Mr. Wilbarger. "I can tell this is going to be a real battle."

Mr. Wilbarger stood up. "Well, I need to get back to the bakery," he said. "Bye, girls."

"Bye," Katie Lynn and Tina said.

"I'll walk you to the door, George," said Grandma. They left the kitchen together.

"Tina!" Katie Lynn said. "Grandma winked at Mr. Wilbarger."

"She probably just had something in her eye," Tina said.

"But she also called him 'George,'" Katie Lynn added.

"Well, maybe that's his name," said Tina.

"That's not what I mean, Tina," said Katie Lynn. "Why didn't she call him 'Mr. Wilbarger'?"

Tina shrugged. She looked at the clock on the wall. "Oh, no! I'm late," she said.

"I have to baby-sit Gerald!"

Katie Lynn followed Tina out.

When they got to the living room, Katie Lynn suddenly pulled Tina back into the kitchen.

"Did you see what I saw?" Katie Lynn gasped.

"What?" said Tina.

"Mr. Wilbarger kissed Grandma on the cheek!" said Katie Lynn.

"Why would he do that?" Tina said.

"Jonathan wants to win the Battle of the Bakers," said Katie Lynn. "His grandfather's probably buttering up Grandma so she'll give away all our secrets."

Chapter 3

Grandma Invites the Enemy Home

The next day after school, Grandma drove Katie Lynn and Tina to the grocery store. They were going to buy the ingredients for their contest cookie. They had decided to bake Grandma's Chocolate Macaroons.

They also needed to buy ingredients for Mr. Chesterfield's next order of cookies. Luckily, Grandma had told them that she would take care of baking those while Katie Lynn and Tina were busy with the contest.

Katie Lynn and Tina pushed the cart through the store.

"Oh, no!" whispered Tina.

She pulled Katie Lynn down behind the bananas.

"What's wrong?" Katie Lynn asked.

Tina peeked over the fruit.

"It's Jonathan and his grandfather!" she whispered. "They're headed this way."

"Hi, George," they heard Grandma say. "Hi, Jonathan."

Katie Lynn stood up.

"What are you doing?" Tina whispered.

"We have nothing to hide," Katie Lynn said.

Tina stood up beside her. "You're right."

"Hi, Jonathan," said Katie Lynn. "Why are you here?"

"I'm buying the ingredients for my bread," Jonathan said. He grinned. "Why were you two hiding? Are you afraid of losing the Battle of the Bakers?"

"We're not afraid of *anything*, Jonathan Wilbarger," Katie Lynn said.

"That's right!" said Tina.

Katie Lynn looked at Grandma for support. But Grandma didn't notice. She was too busy smiling at Mr. Wilbarger.

"How are you today?" Mr. Wilbarger asked Grandma.

"I'm fine," said Grandma. "How are you?"

"I'm fine, too," said Mr. Wilbarger.

For several moments, no one said anything. Grandma didn't stop smiling.

Something is definitely going on, thought Katie Lynn.

Finally, Mr. Wilbarger said, "Well, Jonathan, we need to get the rest of your bread ingredients." He smiled at Grandma. "We'll see you later."

"I hope so," said Grandma.

Katie Lynn pushed the cart into the next aisle.

"I need to talk to the butcher," said Grandma. "Why don't you and Tina get the rest of the ingredients for the cookies?"

"All right, Grandma," said Katie Lynn.

She and Tina headed toward the baking aisle.

"Jonathan Wilbarger makes me so mad," Tina whispered. "Why does he think we're afraid of losing the Battle of the Bakers?"

"Why would we be afraid?" asked Katie Lynn. "We're going to win!"

Suddenly, Jonathan jumped out from behind a tall stack of green-bean cans. "No, you're not!" he said. "I am!" He made a silly face at them. Then he ran down the aisle.

"Oh!" Katie Lynn said. "Can you believe he did that?"

"No, I can't," said Tina.

"Why do all of the cute boys have to act so silly?" said Katie Lynn.

"Yeah!" said Tina. "Why can't they be mature like us?"

Katie Lynn and Tina got the ingredients they needed. Then they met Grandma in the meat market. She was talking to Mr.

Wilbarger. *What is going on here?* Katie Lynn wondered.

"Well, I think we have everything," said Mr. Wilbarger. "I need to find Jonathan so we can go home."

"He's probably hiding behind some cans," grumbled Tina.

Mr. Wilbarger gave her a funny look.

"We're ready to leave, too. So why don't you and Jonathan come by on your way home?" said Grandma. "I'll give you that recipe you asked about."

"Okay," said Mr. Wilbarger.

Oh, no! thought Katie Lynn. *Grandma had invited the enemy home!*

Chapter 4

Disaster!

Grandma drove out of the grocery store parking lot.

Katie Lynn and Tina were in the back seat.

"I wish that Jonathan Wilbarger weren't so cute," whispered Tina. "Then maybe I wouldn't like him so much."

"I know," whispered Katie Lynn. "I can't believe he's coming to my house."

They both let out a big sigh.

"What's wrong, girls?" Grandma asked.

"Grandma, why did you have to invite the Wilbargers over?" Katie Lynn said. "All Jonathan did at the grocery store was tease us."

Grandma smiled. "Well, I'll tell you a little secret," she said. "Boys only tease girls that they like."

"Really?" exclaimed Katie Lynn.

Grandma nodded.

"Then Jonathan must like us a *lot*," said Tina.

Grandma chuckled.

When they got home, Grandma headed toward the kitchen.

"Okay," said Katie Lynn. She turned to Tina. "Now I'm positive that Grandma is giving away our baking secrets."

"Really?" Tina cried.

Katie Lynn nodded. "I don't think she's doing it on purpose. But Mr. Wilbarger asks for recipes. She tells him. Then he tells Jonathan what she says."

"What are we going to do?" asked Tina.

Before Katie Lynn could answer, the doorbell rang.

"I'll get it!" Grandma cried. She ran toward the front door and let Mr. Wilbarger and Jonathan in.

Katie Lynn looked at Tina. "This is so embarrassing," she whispered.

"I know," said Tina.

"Why don't you kids stay in here?" Grandma said. "Mr. Wilbarger and I will visit in the kitchen."

Jonathan sat down in a chair.

Katie Lynn and Tina sat down on the sofa.

They watched Grandma and Mr. Wilbarger disappear through the kitchen door.

"What do you want to talk about, Jonathan?" Tina asked.

Jonathan looked at Katie Lynn. "Is my grandpa giving your grandma our baking secrets?"

Katie Lynn and Tina looked at each other.

"I don't think so," Katie Lynn said. "Besides, we don't need your baking secrets. Is my grandma giving your grandpa *our* baking secrets?"

"I don't think so," Jonathan said. "At least, not yet."

Just then, Grandma and Mr. Wilbarger came back into the living room.

"Mr. Wilbarger is going to give me a tour of the bakery," said Grandma.

Katie Lynn and Jonathan looked at each other.

"You can stay here for a while if you want, Jonathan," said Mr. Wilbarger.

"Okay," Jonathan said.

Grandma and Mr. Wilbarger headed out the front door.

Jonathan turned to Katie Lynn and Tina. "This is our chance," he whispered.

"What do you mean?" asked Katie Lynn.

"I mean, the contest is tomorrow. If they want to give away our secrets, they'll have to do it now."

"Really?" asked Tina.

"I know how we can find out for sure," said Jonathan. "Let's go to the bakery."

Katie Lynn ran to the den. Her parents were watching a cooking show on television. Katie Lynn asked them if she and Tina could go to Jonathan's.

"Okay, dear," said Mrs. Cooke.

"Be careful crossing the street," added Mr. Cooke.

Katie Lynn, Tina, and Jonathan left the house and raced down the street.

When they got to Wilbarger's Bakery, they went to the back door.

"Wait here," Jonathan said. He slipped inside.

In a few minutes, he reappeared. He was holding three white hats, three white coats, and a bag of flour.

"What are those for?" asked Tina.

"This is what all of our workers wear," said Jonathan. "We can use them as disguises."

The three of them hurriedly put on the white hats and the white coats.

"They're kind of big," said Katie Lynn.

"It's all I could find," said Jonathan. "Just roll up the sleeves."

"Don't we need masks, too?" asked Tina. "They'll recognize us if we don't wear masks."

"No, they won't," said Jonathan. He grabbed a handful of flour and threw it at Katie Lynn and Tina.

"What did you do that for?" demanded Tina. "It's all over my face and in my hair."

"I know. But that's what happens when you work in a bakery," said Jonathan. "Now no one will recognize you." He laughed. "Maybe you should wear it more often!"

Before Tina could say anything, Jonathan handed her the bag of flour. "Here. Your turn."

Katie Lynn and Tina each threw a handful of flour at Jonathan.

"Hey! It works. You don't look like

yourself anymore," said Tina.

"Then we're ready," said Jonathan. "Let's go."

He opened the back door. The three of them slipped inside.

The back of the bakery was huge. Everything was made of stainless steel.

"There they are!" Jonathan whispered.

Katie Lynn looked. Grandma and Mr. Wilbarger were on the other side of the bakery. They were looking at the family pictures on the wall.

"Yuck!" said Jonathan. "Why are they looking at those?"

All of a sudden, Mr. Wilbarger whispered something in Grandma's ear.

Grandma giggled.

"We have to get closer!" said Jonathan. "I want to hear what they're saying."

"And I want to see the pictures!" said Tina.

Jonathan dropped to his knees and started crawling. Katie Lynn and Tina did the same thing.

Several of the workers gave them strange looks.

Finally, they reached the other side of the bakery. The only thing that separated them from Grandma and Mr. Wilbarger

now was a huge cart. It was stacked high with loaves of bread.

"We can't let the kids know," said Grandma.

"I know," said Mr. Wilbarger.

Katie Lynn and Jonathan looked at each other.

"Oh, look," said Grandma. "What a cute picture of Jonathan. He's still in diapers!"

Jonathan froze.

"I have to see this!" said Tina. She leaned around the cart.

Jonathan jumped up to block her view. They both banged into the bread.

Everyone fell down in a big pile. The loaves of bread fell on top of them.

"Jonathan Wilbarger!"

Katie Lynn peeked out between two loaves of bread.

Jonathan's grandfather was standing over them. "What in the world is going on here?" he demanded.

Jonathan gulped. "I'm giving Katie Lynn and Tina a tour of the bakery, too."

Chapter 5

Ready for Battle

"Katie Lynn! Wake up!"

Katie Lynn opened her eyes. Tina was standing at the foot of her bed. Katie Lynn yawned. "What time is it?"

"Eight o'clock!" Tina said.

"Eight o'clock!" Katie Lynn cried. She jumped out of bed. "We have to be at the convention center at ten!"

"I know!" Tina said. "Hurry!"

Tina looked in Katie Lynn's mirror. She straightened her dress. "There's no flour left in my hair from yesterday, is there?" she asked.

"No," said Katie Lynn. "Why are you wearing that dress?"

"I want to look nice for Jonathan," Tina replied. "Did you hear how much he was teasing us yesterday?"

"Tina! We're not going to a party. We're baking cookies!" Katie Lynn said. *"And we're trying to beat Jonathan!"*

"I still want to beat him, Katie Lynn," Tina said. "I just want to look nice doing it."

"Well, you're going to get dirty," said Katie Lynn. "You won't look very nice then."

"Oh, I can't get dirty, Katie Lynn," Tina

said. "This is my best dress."

"Then go home and change," Katie Lynn said. "We won't win if you don't."

"Why not?" Tina demanded.

"Because you'll be thinking more about staying clean than baking cookies," Katie Lynn said.

Tina sighed. "Oh, all right," she finally

said. "I'll go home and change."

"Katie Lynn! Tina!" Grandma called from downstairs. "We need to get ready."

"Okay!" said Katie Lynn.

Tina ran home. When she got back, Katie Lynn had everything packed.

Mr. and Mrs. Cooke came into the kitchen.

"Ready?" Mr. Cooke said.

"Yes!" said Grandma. "I think we have everything." She looked at Katie Lynn and Tina. "Let's go to the convention center, girls! It's time to do battle!"

Chapter 6

Bakers, Get Ready!

"Wow!" Tina said. "Look!"

Katie Lynn looked. She saw a long row of kitchens, one right next to the other.

"Each contestant gets to have his or her own kitchen to work in," said Grandma. "We're Number Ten."

"This is great," said Katie Lynn. "Come on. These bags are getting heavy."

They started down the aisle. Some of the other kids were already in their kitchens.

"Girls, your parents are waving to you," said Grandma.

Katie Lynn and Tina looked. They found Mr. and Mrs. Cooke in the audience. Tina's parents and Gerald were there, too. They waved back.

"There's Number Ten!" Tina said. "It's the last one."

Katie Lynn stopped. "Oh, no!" she cried. She turned to Grandma. "Jonathan's kitchen is right next to ours."

"Well, that shouldn't be a problem," said Grandma.

Katie Lynn thought it would be. What if Jonathan started teasing them while they were trying to mix their ingredients?

41

Grandma and Mr. Wilbarger waved at each other.

"Hey, you two!" Jonathan called. He had a big grin on his face. "Why did you show up? You're just gonna get beat!"

"Let's pretend we didn't hear him," Katie Lynn said.

"Yeah!" said Tina. She turned to Jonathan. "We didn't hear you!" she called.

"Tina!" Katie Lynn hissed. "That's not what I meant!"

"I SAID, 'YOU'RE GONNA GET BEAT!'" Jonathan shouted.

Some of the other kids looked out of their kitchens to see what was going on.

"Sometimes I wish he didn't like us so much," said Tina.

"I know exactly what you mean," said Katie Lynn.

They went into their kitchen.

"Who are those people in Jonathan's kitchen?" asked Tina.

Grandma looked. "Oh, those are the judges. They come around to make sure we follow the rules."

Katie Lynn thought the judges looked mean. She just hoped they liked chocolate macaroons.

"They're coming this way," said Tina. "What do we do?"

"You smile and say hello," replied Grandma. "You don't have to do anything else."

The three judges made their way into Katie Lynn's kitchen. They were all carrying clipboards. They had pencils in their hands.

The judges nodded at Katie Lynn, Tina,

and Grandma. But they didn't say anything.

Instead, one judge headed toward the refrigerator. The other two judges headed toward the cabinets. They opened all of the doors and looked inside. Then they wrote down things on their clipboards.

Katie Lynn and Tina gave them a big smile. The judges smiled back. Then they left.

A loudspeaker squawked and squealed.

"ATTENTION, CONTESTANTS!" the loudspeaker squawked. "THE BATTLE OF THE BAKERS IS ABOUT TO BEGIN!"

The crowd cheered.

"Oh, I'm nervous!" Katie Lynn whispered.

"Me too," said Tina.

"Don't be," said Grandma. "Just pretend you're in our kitchen at home."

"TURN ON YOUR OVENS!" the loudspeaker squawked.

Grandma went to the oven and turned it on to 350 degrees Fahrenheit.

Then the loudspeaker squawked again, "BAKERS, GET READY!"

Katie Lynn and Tina each took a deep breath and let it out.

"WAIT!" a voice shouted.

Katie Lynn and Tina looked at each other.

"That sounds like Jonathan," Katie Lynn said.

She and Tina ran around the partition to Jonathan's kitchen. Grandma followed. The judges were already there. They were wringing their hands and whispering.

"What's wrong, Jonathan?" Katie Lynn said.

"My oven won't work," Jonathan said.

"Oh, well, I guess we won, then," said Tina. "You can't bake bread if your oven won't work."

One of the judges turned to them. "Do you know each other?" she asked.

Katie Lynn and Tina nodded.

"What's your oven setting, Jonathan?" one judge asked.

"Three hundred and fifty degrees Fahrenheit," replied Jonathan.

The judge turned to Katie Lynn. "What's yours?"

"The same," Katie Lynn replied.

The judge quickly whispered something

to the other judges. They nodded.

"We've decided it will be okay if you both use the same oven!" the judge said. "You'll be sharing a kitchen!"

Mixing Bowl Mix-up

Grandma helped Mr. Wilbarger and Jonathan carry Jonathan's ingredients and pots and pans over to Katie Lynn and Tina's kitchen.

"I knew I should have worn my pretty dress," Tina muttered. "I knew I shouldn't have changed."

"Do you think Grandma and Mr. Wilbarger planned this?" Katie Lynn whispered.

Tina gasped. "Would they really do

something like that?" she asked.

"I don't know," said Katie Lynn.

Jonathan and Katie Lynn and Tina stood together at the kitchen counter. There was hardly any room to move.

Suddenly, the loudspeaker squawked, "BAKERS, BEGIN BAKING!"

The audience applauded.

"Come on, Jonathan!" several guys shouted.

Jonathan grinned at Katie Lynn and Tina.

"Come on, Katie Lynn and Tina!" several girls cheered.

Katie Lynn and Tina grinned back at Jonathan. Then they hurriedly got out the pots and pans and the ingredients for the cookies.

"Jonathan, your stuff is in the way,"

Katie Lynn complained. "You have to move over. We don't have enough room."

"Well, it's not my fault." Jonathan pushed his things together. "I don't have enough room, either. Besides, this is my kitchen, too," he reminded them.

Katie Lynn and Tina took out pecans, sugar, cocoa, chocolate, salt, eggs, and vanilla for their cookies.

Jonathan took out sugar, butter, eggs, buttermilk, flour, baking powder, baking soda, and salt for his bread.

They started measuring the ingredients and mixing them together in bowls.

"Hey!" Jonathan cried. "That's my sugar!"

"No, it's not," said Katie Lynn. "I put your sugar over there."

"Where's the cocoa?" asked Tina.

"I put it next to the buttermilk," said Jonathan.

Katie Lynn groaned. This was going to be harder than she had thought.

Katie Lynn looked at their recipe. "Break two eggs, Tina," she said.

Tina tried to break two eggs. But she dropped them both on the floor.

Jonathan grinned at Tina. "That's a great recipe, Tina. 'Drop two eggs on the floor.' You'll have to teach me that one."

Tina blushed.

"Quick, Tina!" Katie Lynn said. "I need the cocoa!"

"Here it is," said Tina. "What do I do with it?"

"Dump it in the bowl," said Katie Lynn.

Tina dumped it in the bowl next to her.

"Tina!" Jonathan cried. "What are you doing?"

"I'm putting the cocoa in our mixing bowl," said Tina.

"No, Tina!" Katie Lynn said. "Our mixing bowl is over here."

"That's my bread dough!" Jonathan said.

"What's wrong?" Grandma and Mr. Wilbarger asked.

Katie Lynn told them.

"Oh, Jonathan! I'm sorry," Tina said. She had tears in her eyes. "What kind of bread was it?"

"Buttermilk," Jonathan replied.

Tina tried to smile. "Well, now I guess it's *Chocolate*-Buttermilk Bread," she said. Jonathan didn't say anything.

"It's too late to start over, Jonathan," said Mr. Wilbarger. "You'll have to bake it with the cocoa if you want to finish the contest."

Jonathan had a sad look on his face.

"Hurry, Tina," said Katie Lynn. "We have to finish our cookies. Put a quarter cup of cocoa in our bowl."

Tina looked in the cocoa tin. "There's nothing left," she said.

"What?" cried Katie Lynn.

"I dumped it all in Jonathan's bread," said Tina. Her voice sounded shaky.

"You guys probably planned this!" shouted Jonathan. "I can't believe you would sink so low. You ruined my bread."

"Well, what about our cookies, Jonathan?" Katie Lynn said. "They're ruined, too. We can't make chocolate macaroons if we don't have any cocoa."

The judges rushed into the kitchen.

"What's going on?" said one. "You better start baking if you want a chance at the grand prize!"

Katie Lynn, Tina, and Jonathan stared at the chocolate-buttermilk batter. Then they looked at each other.

"I guess there's only one thing we can do," said Jonathan.

"What?" asked Tina between sniffles.

"Start baking," said Katie Lynn.

Chapter 8

Chocolate-Buttermilk Bread

For the next hour, everyone stood around nervously. No one knew what to say.

Just as the loudspeaker squawked, "TIME'S UP!", the timer dinged.

"Wow!" said Tina. "We made it!"

Grandma and Mr. Wilbarger rushed to the oven. Together, they removed the bread pan.

"It looks good," said Grandma.

"It smells good," said Mr. Wilbarger.

"But whoever heard of Chocolate-Buttermilk Bread?" Jonathan said.

"Don't give up, Jonathan," Katie Lynn said. "The judges haven't even tasted it yet."

"I hope they don't get sick," said Tina.

The judges started judging at Kitchen Number 1.

Slowly, they worked their way down the row of kitchens.

"They won't be hungry by the time they get to us," said Tina. "They won't want to eat our Chocolate-Buttermilk Bread."

"They probably won't want to eat it anyway," said Jonathan.

Finally, the judges reached their kitchen.

"Let's see," one judge said. She was looking at her clipboard. "Is this the bread or the macaroons?"

"Both," said Katie Lynn.

"We kind of had an accident," explained Tina.

"We want to enter it anyway," said Jonathan.

The judge looked at the pan. "Well, what *is* it?" she asked.

"It's Chocolate-Buttermilk Bread," said Katie Lynn.

The judges cut the bread. They each ate a slice.

Katie Lynn, Tina, and Jonathan held their breath.

"Hmm," said one of the judges.

"Interesting," said another.

"Who would have thought?" said the last judge.

The judges left and returned to their seats.

The loudspeaker played music while the judges made their decision.

Suddenly, the music stopped. The loudspeaker squawked, "THE WINNERS HAVE BEEN CHOSEN."

Katie Lynn, Tina, and Jonathan looked at each other. Jonathan took hold of Katie Lynn's and Tina's hands.

Katie Lynn blushed. So did Tina.

"THE THIRD PRIZE GOES TO THE PUDGY FUDGY BROWNIES FROM KITCHEN SEVEN."

The audience applauded.

"THE SECOND PRIZE GOES TO CHARLIE'S CHEESY CHEESECAKE FROM KITCHEN THREE."

The audience applauded some more.

"They didn't like ours," Tina said. "It was all my fault." Tears started streaming down her face.

Katie Lynn squeezed her hand.

"THIS HAS NEVER HAPPENED BEFORE. THE WINNER IS NOT JUST ONE ENTRY. IT'S A COMBINATION

OF TWO. THE SECRET GRAND PRIZE GOES TO...THE CHOCOLATE-BUTTERMILK BREAD FROM KITCH-EN TEN!"

Katie Lynn, Tina, and Jonathan started screaming. They jumped up and down.

"I knew we'd win!" Tina cried. "I knew we'd win!"

Mr. and Mrs. Cooke rushed into the kitchen. They hugged Tina and Katie Lynn. They were followed by Gerald and Tina's parents.

"I wonder what the secret grand prize is," Jonathan whispered. "I hope it's a new car."

"We can't drive, Jonathan," said Tina.

"That's okay," said Jonathan. "I'll keep it in my garage until I can."

"Why would you keep it in *your* garage,

Jonathan?" asked Katie Lynn. "It would belong to me and Tina, too."

"Oh, yeah," said Jonathan.

"Well, I hope it's new clothes," said Tina.

"Yuck!" said Jonathan.

The loudspeaker squawked, "THE SECRET GRAND PRIZE IS A TRIP TO NEW YORK CITY TO APPEAR ON *THE BETSY BAKER SHOW!*"

"The Betsy Baker Show!" cried Katie Lynn. "That's wonderful!"

Suddenly, all three judges rushed into the kitchen. "Congratulations! Could we please have some more of that Chocolate-Buttermilk Bread? It's delicious!" they said.

Grandma cut them three more slices.

"Who's Betsy Baker?" Jonathan asked.

"Jonathan! You've never heard of Betsy Baker?" Tina said. "She's just the best cook on television!"

"You mean we could be television stars?" Jonathan said.

"Yes!" said one of the judges. She was cutting herself another slice of bread. "But you won't be on the show for several months."

"Good! I want to change my hairstyle," said Tina. "I have to look just right for my television debut."

"What a great surprise!" said Katie Lynn.

Grandma turned to Mr. Wilbarger. "We have another surprise for you," she said.

"You do?" said Katie Lynn.

Grandma nodded. "Mr. Wilbarger and I are getting married!"

Katie Lynn and Jonathan stared at each other. "Married?" they said.

Tina grinned. "Katie Lynn! That means Jonathan can't tease you anymore!" Tina said.

"What are you talking about?" Jonathan asked.

"Well, everyone knows that boys only tease girls if they like them," said Tina. "You can't *like* someone you're related to."

"Well, I've never heard that before," Jonathan said. "But I have heard that it's all right to tease relatives." He made a face at Katie Lynn. She laughed and made a face back.

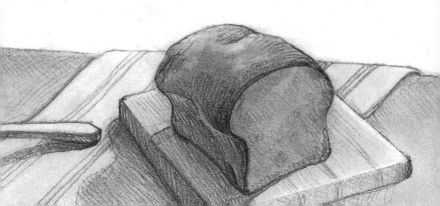

"Why didn't you tell us, Grandma?" she asked.

"We didn't want to distract you during the contest," Mr. Wilbarger said.

"We didn't want you to worry that we were giving away baking secrets or anything silly like that!" Grandma said.

Katie Lynn, Tina, and Jonathan looked at each other.

"We'd never think anything like that, Grandma," Katie Lynn said quickly.

"No! Never!" Tina and Jonathan chimed in.

"Good," said Grandma. "Because, Katie Lynn, we want you and Tina to be our flower girls."

"Yes!" said Katie Lynn.

"I'll get a new dress!" said Tina.

"Jonathan can be our ring bearer," said Mr. Wilbarger.

"And we'll all help make the cookies, Grandma," said Katie Lynn. She looked at Jonathan and Tina. *"Wedding cookies!"*

Katie Lynn's Cookbook

THE SECRET GRAND PRIZE–WINNING RECIPE

CHOCOLATE-BUTTERMILK BREAD

  1 CUP SUGAR

  1/2 CUP (ONE STICK) SOFTENED BUTTER
  (TO SOFTEN THE BUTTER, TAKE IT
  OUT OF THE REFRIGERATOR AT LEAST
  ONE HOUR BEFORE USING.)

  2 EGGS

  1 CUP BUTTERMILK

  1 3/4 CUPS ALL-PURPOSE FLOUR

  1/2 CUP UNSWEETENED COCOA

  1/2 TEASPOON BAKING POWDER

  1/2 TEASPOON BAKING SODA

  1/2 TEASPOON SALT

Get a grownup to preheat the oven to 350 degrees Fahrenheit.

Grease the bottom of a 9 x 5-inch loaf pan. (You can also use a cooking spray.)

Put the sugar and the butter in a large bowl and mix well by hand (or with a mixer).

Add the eggs and beat together well.

Then stir in the buttermilk.

Add the flour, the cocoa, the baking powder, the baking soda, and the salt. Stir until the dry ingredients are just moistened. Put the batter in the loaf pan.

Bake at 350 degrees Fahrenheit for 55 to 65 minutes. (It's done when a toothpick inserted into the center comes out clean!) Cool for 15 minutes.

Slice and serve. The bread is great with strawberry or cherry preserves or raspberry jam.

Katie Lynn's Cookbook

GRANDMA'S CHOCOLATE MACAROONS

1 CUP GROUND PECANS

1 CUP SUGAR

1/4 CUP UNSWEETENED COCOA

1 SQUARE UNSWEETENED CHOCOLATE, CHOPPED

1/8 TEASPOON SALT

2 LARGE EGG WHITES

1 TEASPOON VANILLA

Get a grownup to preheat the oven to 350 degrees Fahrenheit.

Line a large cookie sheet with ungreased aluminum foil.

In a large bowl, mix together by hand

the ground pecans, the sugar, the cocoa, the chocolate, and the salt.

Get a grownup to help separate the egg yolks from the egg whites. Then add the egg whites and the vanilla and mix by hand until well blended.

Scoop up the dough with a teaspoon and drop it onto the cookie sheet two inches apart.

Bake the cookies for at least ten minutes.

Let them cool for about five minutes.

Hungry for More?
Don't Miss These Tempting Titles!

The Katie Lynn Cookie Company #1:
The Secret Ingredient

Katie Lynn knows cookies, but does she have what it takes to run her own business?

The Katie Lynn Cookie Company #2:
Frogs' Legs for Dinner?

Can the Katie Lynn Cookie Company survive too many cooks in the kitchen?

The Katie Lynn Cookie Company #3:
The Battle of the Bakers

The heat is on when Katie Lynn, Tina, and Jonathan all enter the town's baking contest.

And coming soon…

The Katie Lynn Cookie Company

Book #4
Wedding Cookies

Can Katie Lynn's cookies stop a wedding day disaster?

ABOUT THE AUTHOR

G. E. STANLEY is the author of more than fifty books for young people, many of them award winners. He and his wife, Gwen, live in Lawton, Oklahoma. They have two sons, Charles and James, a daughter-in-law, Tambye, and a family dog, a Labrador retriever named Daisy.

"I'll never forget the first battle I had in the kitchen," says G. E. Stanley. "I made the mistake of telling my sister, JoAnn, that I was a better cook than she was. I honestly don't remember who threw the first handful of flour, but pretty soon we were having a *real* 'battle of the bakers.' Flour was everywhere, and suddenly we realized that the only contest we needed to have was to see who could clean up the kitchen the fastest before our parents got home!"